ALICE DUNBAR NELSON

Alice Dunbar Nelson was born in New Orleans in 1875. Of mixed descent, she grew up amongst Creole society, and her upbringing informs much of her fiction. She graduated as a teacher and taught in schools through much of her life. She was also a published poet, journalist, public speaker and activist, and she became a key figure of the Harlem Renaissance. Her first book, an anthology of prose and poetry, *Violets and Other Tales*, was published in 1895, and her acclaimed short-story collection, *The Goodness of St. Rocque and Other Stories*, followed in 1899. Her first marriage, to the poet Paul Laurence Dunbar, was short. She remarried twice, first to Henry Arthur Callis, a doctor, and then to journalist and politician Robert J. Nelson. She died in Philadelphia in 1935.

ALICE DUNBAR NELSON

A Carnival Jangle

M
10

'The Fisherman of Pass Christian', 'M'sieu Fortier's Violin', 'Sister Josepha', 'Little Miss Sophie',
'Odalie' and 'The Goodness of St. Rocque' first published in
The Goodness of St. Rocque and Other Stories 1899
'Summer Session' and 'His Great Career' first published 1993
'A Carnival Jangle' first published in *Violets and Other Tales* 1895

This edition first published 2026 by Macmillan Collector's Library
an imprint of Pan Macmillan
The Smithson, 6 Briset Street, London EC1M 5NR
EU representative: Macmillan Publishers Ireland Ltd, 1st Floor,
The Liffey Trust Centre, 117–126 Sheriff Street Upper,
Dublin 1 D01 YC43
Associated companies throughout the world

ISBN 978-1-0374-0341-5

1 3 5 7 9 8 6 4 2

A CIP catalogue record for this book is available from the British Library.

Cover design: Tiana-Jane Dunlop, Pan Macmillan Art Department
Typeset in Adobe Caslon Pro by Six Red Marbles UK, Thetford, Norfolk
Printed and bound in the UK using 100% Renewable Electricity by CPI Group (UK) Ltd

CONTENTS

The Fisherman of Pass Christian

The swift breezes on the beach at Pass Christian meet and conflict as though each strove for the mastery of the air. The land-breeze blows down through the pines, resinous, fragrant, cold, bringing breath-like memories of dim, dark woods shaded by myriad pine-needles. The breeze from the Gulf is warm and soft and languorous, blowing up from the south with its suggestion of tropical warmth and passion. It is strong and masterful, and tossed Annette's hair and whipped her skirts about her in bold disregard for the proprieties.

Arm in arm with Philip, she was strolling slowly down the great pier which extends from the Mexican Gulf Hotel into the waters of the Sound. There was no moon to-night, but the sky glittered and scintillated with myriad stars, brighter than you can ever see farther North, and the great waves that the Gulf breeze tossed up in restless profusion gleamed with the white fire of phosphorescent flame. The wet sands on the beach glowed white fire; the posts of the pier where the waves had leapt and left a laughing kiss, the sides of the little boats and fish-cars tugging at their ropes, alike showed white and flaming, as though the sea and all it touched were afire.

Annette and Philip paused midway the pier to watch

two fishermen casting their nets. With heads bared to the breeze, they stood in clear silhouette against the white background of sea.

"See how he uses his teeth," almost whispered Annette.

Drawing himself up to his full height, with one end of the huge seine between his teeth, and the cord in his left hand, the taller fisherman of the two paused a half instant, his right arm extended, grasping the folds of the net. There was a swishing rush through the air, and it settled with a sort of sob as it cut the waters and struck a million sparkles of fire from the waves. Then, with backs bending under the strain, the two men swung on the cord, drawing in the net, laden with glittering restless fish, which were unceremoniously dumped on the boards to be put into the fish-car awaiting them.

Philip laughingly picked up a soft, gleaming jellyfish, and threatened to put it on Annette's neck. She screamed, ran, slipped on the wet boards, and in another instant would have fallen over into the water below. The tall fisherman caught her in his arms and set her on her feet.

"Mademoiselle must be very careful," he said in the softest and most correct French. "The tide is in and the water very rough. It would be very difficult to swim out there to-night."

Annette murmured confused thanks, which were supplemented by Philip's hearty tones. She was silent until they reached the pavilion at the end of the pier. The semi-darkness was unrelieved by lantern or light. The strong wind wafted the strains from a couple of mandolins, a guitar, and a tenor voice stationed in one corner to sundry engrossed couples in sundry other corners. Philip found an untenanted nook and they ensconced themselves therein.

"Do you know there's something mysterious about that fisherman?" said Annette, during a lull in the wind.

"Because he did not let you go over?" inquired Philip.

"No; he spoke correctly, and with the accent that goes only with an excellent education."

Philip shrugged his shoulders. "That's nothing remarkable. If you stay about Pass Christian for any length of time, you'll find more things than perfect French and courtly grace among fishermen to surprise you. These are a wonderful people who live across the Lake."

Annette was lolling in the hammock under the big catalpa-tree some days later, when the gate opened, and Natalie's big sun-bonnet appeared. Natalie herself was discovered blushing in its dainty depths. She was only a little Creole seaside girl, you must know, and very shy of the city demoiselles. Natalie's patois was quite as different from Annette's French as it was from the postmaster's English.

"Mees Annette," she began, peony-hued all over at her own boldness, "we will have one lil' hay-ride this night, and a fish-fry at the end. Will you come?"

Annette sprang to her feet in delight. "Will I come? Certainly. How delightful! You are so good to ask me. What shall—what time—" But Natalie's pink bonnet had fled precipitately down the shaded walk. Annette laughed joyously as Philip lounged down the gallery.

"I frightened the child away," she told him.

You've never been for a hay-ride and fish-fry on the shores of the Mississippi Sound, have you? When the summer boarders and the Northern visitors undertake to give one, it is a comparatively staid affair, where due regard is had for one's wearing apparel, and where there are servants to do the hardest work. Then it isn't enjoyable at all. But when the natives, the boys and girls who live there, make up their minds to have fun, you may depend upon its being just the best kind.

This time there were twenty boys and girls, a mamma or so, several papas, and a grizzled fisherman to restrain the ardor of the amateurs. The cart was vast and solid, and two comfortable, sleepy-looking mules constituted the drawing power. There were also tin horns, some guitars, an accordeon, and a quartet of much praised voices. The hay in the bottom of the wagon was freely mixed with pine needles, whose prickiness through your hose was amply compensated for by its delicious fragrance.

After a triumphantly noisy passage down the beach one comes to the stretch of heavy sand that lies between Pass Christian proper and Henderson's Point. This is a hard pull for the mules, and the more ambitious riders get out and walk. Then, after a final strain through the shifting sands, bravo! the shell road is reached, and one goes cheering through the pine-trees to Henderson's Point.

If ever you go to Pass Christian, you must have a fish-fry at Henderson's Point. It is the pine-thicketed, white-beached peninsula jutting out from the land, with one side caressed by the waters of the Sound and the other purred over by the blue waves of the Bay of St. Louis. Here is the beginning of the great three-mile trestle bridge to the town of Bay St. Louis, and to-night from the beach could be seen the lights of the villas glittering across the Bay like myriads of unsleeping eyes.

Here upon a firm stretch of white sand camped the merry-makers. Soon a great fire of driftwood and pine cones tossed its flames defiantly at a radiant moon in the sky, and the fishers were casting their nets in the sea. The more daring of the girls waded bare-legged in the water, holding pine-torches, spearing flounders and peering for soft-shell crabs.

Annette had wandered farther in the shallow water than the rest. Suddenly she stumbled against a stone, the torch dropped and spluttered at her feet. With a little helpless cry she looked at the stretch of unfamiliar beach and water to find herself all alone.

"Pardon me, mademoiselle," said a voice at her elbow; "you are in distress?"

It was her fisherman, and with a scarce conscious sigh of relief, Annette put her hand into the outstretched one at her side.

"I was looking for soft shells," she explained, "and lost the crowd, and now my torch is out."

"Where is the crowd?" There was some amusement in the tone, and Annette glanced up quickly, prepared to be thoroughly indignant at this fisherman who dared make fun at her; but there was such a kindly look about his mouth that she was reassured and said meekly,—

"At Henderson's Point."

"You have wandered a half-mile away," he mused,

"and have nothing to show for your pains but very wet skirts. If mademoiselle will permit me, I will take her to her friends, but allow me to suggest that mademoiselle will leave the water and walk on the sands."

"But I am barefoot," wailed Annette, "and I am afraid of the fiddlers."

Fiddler crabs, you know, aren't pleasant things to be dangling around one's bare feet, and they are more numerous than sand fleas down at Henderson's Point.

"True," assented the fisherman; "then we shall have to wade back."

The fishing was over when they rounded the point and came in sight of the cheery bonfire with its Rembrandt-like group, and the air was savoury with the smell of frying fish and crabs. The fisherman was not to be tempted by appeals to stay, but smilingly disappeared down the sands, the red glare of his torch making a glowing track in the water.

"Ah, Mees Annette," whispered Natalie, between mouthfuls of a rich croaker, "you have found a beau in the water."

"And the fisherman of the Pass, too," laughed her cousin Ida.

Annette tossed her head, for Philip had growled audibly.

"Do you know, Philip," cried Annette a few days after, rudely shaking him from his siesta on the gallery,—"do you know that I have found my fisherman's hut?"

"Hum," was the only response.

"Yes, and it's the quaintest, most delightful spot imaginable. Philip, do come with me and see it."

"Hum."

"Oh, Philip, you are so lazy; do come with me."

"Yes, but, my dear Annette," protested Philip, "this is a warm day, and I am tired."

Still, his curiosity being aroused, he went grumbling. It was not a very long drive, back from the beach across the railroad and through the pine forest to the bank of a dark, slow-flowing bayou. The fisherman's hut was small, two-roomed, whitewashed, pine-boarded, with the traditional mud chimney acting as a sort of support to one of its uneven sides. Within was a weird assortment of curios from every uncivilized part of the globe. Also were there fishing-tackle and guns in reckless profusion. The fisherman, in the kitchen of the mud-chimney, was sardonically waging war with a basket of little bayou crabs.

"Entrez, mademoiselle et monsieur," he said pleasantly, grabbing a vicious crab by its flippers, and smiling at its wild attempts to bite. "You see I am busy, but make yourself at home."

"Well, how on earth—" began Philip.

"Sh—sh—" whispered Annette. "I was driving out in the woods this morning, and stumbled on the hut. He asked me in, but I came right over after you."

The fisherman, having succeeded in getting the last crab in the kettle of boiling water, came forward smiling and began to explain the curios.

"Then you have not always lived at Pass Christian," said Philip.

"Mais non, monsieur, I am spending a summer here."

"And he spends his winters, doubtless, selling fish in the French market," spitefully soliloquised Philip.

The fisherman was looking unutterable things into Annette's eyes, and, it seemed to Philip, taking an unconscionably long time explaining the use of an East Indian stiletto.

"Oh, wouldn't it be delightful!" came from Annette at last.

"What?" asked Philip.

"Why, Monsieur LeConte says he'll take six of us out in his catboat tomorrow for a fishing-trip on the Gulf."

"Hum," drily.

"And I'll get Natalie and her cousins."

"Yes," still more drily.

Annette chattered on, entirely oblivious of the strainedness of the men's adieux, and still chattered as they drove through the pines.

"I did not know that you were going to take fishermen and marchands into the bosom of your social set when you came here," growled Philip, at last.

"But, Cousin Phil, can't you see he is a gentleman? Thc fact that he makes no excuses or protestations is a proof."

"You are a fool," was the polite response.

Still, at six o'clock next morning, there was a little crowd of seven upon the pier, laughing and chatting at the little "Virginie" dipping her bows in the water and flapping her sails in the brisk wind. Natalie's pink bonnet blushed in the early sunshine, and Natalie's mamma, comely and portly, did chaperonage duty. It was not long before the sails gave swell into the breeze and the little boat scurried to the Sound. Past the lighthouse on its gawky iron stalls, she flew, and now rounded the white sands of Cat Island.

"Bravo, the Gulf!" sang a voice on the lookout. The little boat dipped, halted an instant, then rushed fast into the blue Gulf waters.

"We will anchor here," said the host, "have luncheon, and fish."

Philip could not exactly understand why the fisherman should sit so close to Annette and whisper so much into her ears. He chafed at her acting the part of hostess, and was possessed of a murderous desire to throw the pink sun-bonnet and its owner into the sea, when Natalie whispered audibly to one of her cousins that "Mees Annette act nice wit' her lovare."

The sun was banking up flaming pillars of rose and gold in the west when the little "Virginie" rounded Cat Island on her way home, and the quick Southern twilight was fast dying into darkness when she was tied up to the pier and the merry-makers sprang off with baskets of fish. Annette had distinguished herself by catching one small shark, and had immediately ceased to fish and devoted her attention to her fisherman and his line. Philip had angled fiercely, landing trout, croakers, sheepshead, snappers in bewildering luck. He had broken each hopeless captive's neck savagely, as though they were personal enemies. He did not look happy as they landed, though pæans of praise were being sung in his honour.

As the days passed on, "the fisherman of the Pass" began to dance attendance on Annette. What had seemed a joke became serious. Aunt Nina, urged by

Philip, remonstrated, and even the mamma of the pink sun-bonnet began to look grave. It was all very well for a city demoiselle to talk with a fisherman and accept favours at his hands, provided that the city demoiselle understood that a vast and bridgeless gulf stretched between her and the fisherman. But when the demoiselle forgot the gulf and the fisherman refused to recognise it, why, it was time to take matters in hand.

To all of Aunt Nina's remonstrances, Philip's growlings, and the averted glances of her companions, Annette was deaf. "You are narrow-minded," she said laughingly. "I am interested in Monsieur LeConte simply as a study. He is entertaining; he talks well of his travels, and as for refusing to recognise the difference between us, why, he never dreamed of such a thing."

Suddenly a peremptory summons home from Annette's father put an end to the fears of Philip. Annette pouted, but papa must be obeyed. She blamed Philip and Aunt Nina for telling tales, but Aunt Nina was uncommunicative, and Philip too obviously cheerful to derive much satisfaction from.

That night she walked with the fisherman hand in hand on the sands. The wind from the pines bore the scarcely recognisable, subtle freshness of early autumn, and the waters had a hint of dying summer in their sob on the beach.

"You will remember," said the fisherman, "that I have told you nothing about myself."

"Yes," murmured Annette.

"And you will keep your promises to me?"

"Yes."

"Let me hear you repeat them again."

"I promise you that I will not forget you. I promise you that I will never speak of you to anyone until I see you again. I promise that I will then clasp your hand wherever you may be."

"And mademoiselle will not be discouraged, but will continue her studies?"

"Yes."

It was all very romantic, by the waves of the Sound, under a harvest moon, that seemed all sympathy for these two, despite the fact that it was probably looking down upon hundreds of other equally romantic couples. Annette went to bed with glowing cheeks, and a heart whose pulsations would have caused a physician to prescribe unlimited digitalis.

It was still hot in New Orleans when she returned home, and it seemed hard to go immediately to work. But if one is going to be an opera-singer some day and capture the world with one's voice, there is nothing to do but to study, study, sing, practise, even though one's throat be parched, one's head a great ache, and one's heart a nest of discouragement and sadness at what seems the uselessness of it all. Annette had now a new incentive to work; the fisherman had once praised her voice when she hummed a barcarole on the sands, and he had insisted that there was power in its rich notes. Though the fisherman had showed no cause why he should be accepted as a musical critic, Annette had somehow respected his judgment and been accordingly elated.

*

It was the night of the opening of the opera. There was the usual crush, the glitter and confusing radiance of the brilliant audience. Annette, with papa, Aunt Nina, and Philip, was late reaching her box. The curtain was up, and "La Juive" was pouring forth defiance at her angry persecutors. Annette listened breathlessly. In fancy, she too was ringing her voice out to an applauding house. Her head unconsciously beat time to the music, and one hand half held her cloak from her bare shoulders.

Then Eleazar appeared, and the house rose at the end of his song. Encores it gave, and bravos and cheers. He bowed calmly, swept his eyes over the tiers until they found Annette, where they rested in a half-smile of recognition.

"Philip," gasped Annette, nervously raising her glasses, "my fisherman!"

"Yes, an opera-singer is better than a marchand," drawled Philip.

The curtain fell on the first act. The house was won by the new tenor; it called and recalled him before the curtain. Clearly he had sung his way into the hearts of his audience at once.

"Papa, Aunt Nina," said Annette, "you must come behind the scenes with me. I want you to meet him. He is delightful. You must come."

Philip was bending ostentatiously over the girl in the next box. Papa and Aunt Nina consented to be dragged behind the scenes. Annette was well known, for, in hopes of some day being an occupant of one of the dressing-rooms, she had made friends with everyone connected with the opera.

Eleazar received them, still wearing his brown garb and patriarchal beard.

"How you deceived me!" she laughed, when the greetings and introductions were over.

"I came to America early," he smiled back at her, "and thought I'd try a little incognito at the Pass. I was not well, you see. It has been of great benefit to me."

"I kept my promise," she said in a lower tone.

"Thank you; that also has helped me."

Annette's teacher began to note a wonderful improvement in his pupil's voice. Never did a girl study so hard or practise so faithfully. It was truly wonderful. Now and then Annette would say to papa as if to reassure herself,—

"And when Monsieur Cherbart says I am ready to go to Paris, I may go, papa?"

And papa would say a "Certainly" that would send her back to the piano with renewed ardour.

As for Monsieur LeConte, he was the idol of New Orleans. Seldom had there been a tenor who had sung himself so completely into the very hearts of a populace. When he was billed, the opera displayed "Standing Room" signs, no matter what the other attractions in the city might be. Sometimes Monsieur LeConte delighted small audiences in Annette's parlour, when the hostess was in a perfect flutter of happiness. Not often, you know, for the leading tenor was in great demand at the homes of society queens.

"Do you know," said Annette, petulantly, one evening, "I wish for the old days at Pass Christian."

"So do I," he answered tenderly; "will you repeat them with me next summer?"

"If I only could!" she gasped.

Still she might have been happy, had it not been for Madame Dubeau,—Madame Dubeau, the flute-voiced leading soprano, who wore the single dainty curl on her forehead, and thrilled her audiences oftentimes more completely than the fisherman. Madame Dubeau was La Juive to his Eleazar, Leonore to his Manfred, Elsa to his Lohengrin, Aida to his Rhadames, Marguerite to his Faust; in brief, Madame Dubeau was his opposite. She caressed him as Mignon, pleaded with him as Michaela, died for him in "Les Huguenots," broke her heart for love of him in "La Favorite." How could he help but love her, Annette asked herself, how could he? Madame Dubeau was beautiful and gifted and charming.

Once she whispered her fears to him when there was the meagrest bit of an opportunity. He laughed. "You don't understand, little one," he said tenderly; "the relations of professional people to each other are peculiar. After you go to Paris, you will know."

Still, New Orleans had built up its romance, and gossiped accordingly.

"Have you heard the news?" whispered Lola to Annette, leaning from her box at the opera one night. The curtain had just gone up on "Herodias," and for some reason or other, the audience applauded with more warmth than usual. There was a noticeable number of good-humoured, benignant smiles on the faces of the applauders.

"No," answered Annette, breathlessly,—"no, indeed,

Lola; I am going to Paris next week. I am so delighted I can't stop to think."

"Yes, that is excellent," said Lola, "but all New Orleans is smiling at the romance. Monsieur LeConte and Madame Dubeau were quietly married last night, but it leaked out this afternoon. See all the applause she's receiving!"

Annette leaned back in her chair, very white and still. Her box was empty after the first act, and a quiet little tired voice that was almost too faint to be heard in the carriage on the way home, said—

"Papa, I don't think I care to go to Paris, after all."

Summer Session

"You were flirting with him!"

"I was not. I don't know how to flirt."

"So you say, but you can put up a pretty good imitation."

"You're mistaken."

"I am not. And a man you never saw before in your life. And a common taxi driver."

"He's not a common taxi driver."

"How do you know?"

"I just know."

"Strange exchange of intimacies for the first meeting."

"I tell you—"

"Shut up!"

"I won't shut up, and don't you dare tell me that again!"

There was a warning note in her usually gentle voice; an ominous tightening of her soft lips; a steely glint in her violet eyes. Logan heeded the warning and sat in grim silence, while Elise ground gears and otherwise mishandled her little car through the snarled traffic of Amsterdam Avenue.

"You told me 114th Street, and I waited for you there for a half hour, and I got jammed in the traffic and things went wrong, and this young man got out of his taxi, and straightened me out. And while I waited for you he just stayed and talked."

"To your delight."

"What was I to do? Push him away from the running board? I was standing still, and I couldn't drive away since I was waiting for you."

"I told you 115th Street, and there I stood on the corner in the broiling sun for a half hour, while you were carrying on a flirtation with a taxi driver, until I walked back, thinking you might have had an accident."

"Don't you say flirtation to me again. You said 114th Street. You never speak plain over the telephone anyhow."

"Anything else wrong with me since you've met your new friend—The Taxi Adonis?"

Elise brought the car to a grinding, screeching pause in front of the movie house which was their objective. They sat through the two hours of feature and news and cartoons and comedy and prevues in stony silence. They ate a grim meal together in the usual cafeteria, and she set him down at the men's dormitory of the university in the same polite and frigid silence. Logan glanced at her now and then just a trifle apprehensively. He had never seen just this trace of hardness in her, like the glint of unexpected steel beneath soft chiffon. But his manly dignity would not permit him to unbend. He answered her cold good-night with one as cold, and for the first time in that summer session, during which they had grown to know and like one another, they parted without making a future date.

He waited for her next day at luncheon hour, as she

came from her class with a half dozen other chattering summer-school teacher-students. His manner was graciously condescending.

"Shall we have luncheon together?" Lordly and superior as usual.

She flashed her usual violet-eyed smile of delight, but he felt, rather than saw, that the smile did not quite reach the eyes; that the violets were touched as by premature frost.

"What I can't quite understand," he pursued, after he had brought her tray, deftly removed the salad, tea, and crackers, and placed the tray behind the next chair, "is, if you are skillful enough to drive from Portland, Maine, to New York alone and without disaster, how you can get mixed up in a mere traffic jam on Amsterdam Avenue, and have to have a taxi driver get you out."

Elise's brows went up at the awkward English, so at variance with his usual meticulous and precise phrasing, and a haunting query clouded her eyes. Logan quenched an embarrassed "Hem" in iced tea.

"I did not drive from Portland," was her final response. "I came from my own town, twenty-seven miles beyond Portland."

There was no particular reason for Elise's driving down Amsterdam Avenue after classes that afternoon, but she did and a friendly red light brought her to a halt at 114th Street. Adonis—Logan's sneering cognomen stuck in her mind, and she realized with a guilty start how ruggedly applicable it was—stuck his face in her car window. Poppies suffused her cheeks and dewey violets swam in a sea of flame.

"All right?" he queried.

"Quite, thank you." The light was happily yellow, and she meshed her gears.

"What's the hurry?" He put a protesting hand on the wheel.

"I have an engagement!" She sped away frantically. Adonis whistled at the wabbling career of her little coupé down the street.

She saw him just ahead of her in the cafeteria line next evening at dinner time. She reached for her tray with hands that insisted upon trembling, though she shook them angrily. He smiled daringly back at her. He was even handsomer out of his taxi uniform than in it, and the absence of the cap revealed crisp auburn curls of undoubted pugnaciousness.

"You get a seat, I'll bring your dinner."

"But I—"

"Go on—"

There was a difference between Adonis' ordering of her movements and that of Logan's. A sureness of merry audacity against prim didacticism. Shc sat at a window table and meekly arranged silver napkins.

"But I could never eat all that," she protested at the tray, "Beef and potatoes and—and—all that food."

"I knew that's what's the trouble—diet of salads and iced tea and crackers, mentally, spiritually, physically."

Elise ate roast beef and corn on the cob and pie à la mode and laughed at Adonis' jokes, and his whimsical descriptions of man and his appetites. Over their cigarettes she chuckled at his deft characterizations of their fellow diners.

"Eat hay and think hay," he was saying, "thin diets and thin souls. You need a red-blooded chap like me to make you eat food, put flesh on your bones and reconstruct your thinking from New England inhibitions to New York acceptance and enjoyment of life."

Elise's world rocked. School principals used muddled English. Taxi drivers talked like college professors.

Adonis paused and regarded something on his shoulder as if it were a tarantula. Logan's hand quivered in rage, and veins stood up on its pallor "like long blue whips," Elise found herself thinking.

"Aren't you taking a lot of liberties with a young lady to whom you've not been introduced?" snarled the owner of pallor and veins.

Adonis brushed off the hand and the remark with a careless gesture. He arose and bowed elaborately. "Miss Stone and I have been introduced, thank you, by ourselves—and you?"

Elise looked perilously near tears, "Oh, er—Logan—Mr. Long—this is—er—Mr. McShane."

Logan looked stonily through Adonis, "I don't accept introductions to taxi drivers, even if you do eat with them, Elise."

"Oh, please—" she began.

"That's all right," Adonis gathered up the checks. "Just let me settle this with the cashier, and then if you don't mind, we'll go outside, and settle the physical difference between a taxi driver and—" He did not finish the sentence, but the sinister drawl and contemptuous pause made Elise's scalp prickle with shame for Logan.

"You would suggest a common brawl; quite true to

type. I hope, Elise, you have seen enough of such ruffianly conduct to be satisfied."

"Quite the contrary," she answered coolly, "I am going out with Mr. McShane in his taxi." It was pure spite, and she had a sinking feeling that she might not be wanted.

"Terry to you," he retorted, "and let's be going. We've got a busy evening before us."

Logan was beside them on the sidewalk, blocking the way to the taxi parked at the curb.

"Elise, don't be a fool." He grasped her arm and wrenched it, so that she gave an involuntary cry of pain. Terence McShane's next three moves were so violently consecutive as to seem simultaneous. His right hand caught Logan neatly on the point of the chin, so that he went down with amazing swiftness; his left encircled Elise's waist and lifted her into the taxi, and both hands swung the machine with a roar and sputter in the general direction of the Washington bridge.

"But you're losing fares," Elise protested.

"Nonsense. If you can stand this bumpety-bump, what's the dif?"

"It's entrancing," she murmured at the river, the sky, the stars, the electric signs on the Jersey shore, at Terry's hatless curls.

"Police call," the radio protested, "calling all police cars. Look out for taxi license Y327D. Driver abducted summer school student. Watch for taxi. Arrest driver. Kidnapping charge."

From their leafy shelter, where somehow the taxi had parked itself—neither could have told when or how it stopped under those particularly umbrageous trees, they stared at the radio's accusing dial.

"Well, I'll be—" Terry swore softly, "What do you think of that worm putting in such a charge at headquarters?"

"Oh, Terry, you'll be arrested and put in jail!"

"Will you go to jail with me?"

"You know I will—oh, what am I saying?"

"Words of wisdom, me darlin'. Let's go. Anyhow I'm glad we didn't cross the bridge and get into Jersey."

Through circuitous ways and dark streets, avoiding police, taxis, inquisitive small boys and reporters on the loose, they drew up in front of police headquarters.

Elise sat demurely on a bench, and began to repair damages to her hair, complexion, and neck frills. The little pocket mirror wavered ever so slightly as Logan stood accusingly in front of her, but her eyes did not leave the scrutiny of their mirrored counterpart.

"A pretty mess you've made of your life and reputation," he thundered. "Your chances for any position in my school are gone."

Elise put back a refractory curl behind her ear, then tried it out on her cheek again, surveying it critically in the mirror.

"Won't you recommend me for a job, Mr. Principal, after I've studied so hard all summer?"

Terry's gales of unrestrained mirth at the desk made them both look up in amazement. Laughter rocked the walls of the station house, rolled out into the summer street. Captain and Sergeant and Lieutenant and just plain officers roared lustily, all save one quiet plain-clothes man, who laid an iron grip on Logan's arm.

"Terence McShane, you were always the best detective in the city," roared the Captain. "And you made him bring himself right into our outstretched arms."

The iron grip on Logan's arm terminated into steel bracelets.

"Okeh, Longjim Webb, alias Prof. Logan Long, the school principal, looking the summer students over for teaching material in his consolidated upstate school, we'll give you a chance in the Big House to meditate on the law against white slavery."

"Your zeal to corral this particular choice bit of femininity made you throw caution to the winds," suggested Detective Terence McShane.

Incredulity, disgust, anger swept the violet eyes. Elise flared into Terry's face.

"You—you—pretending to be a taxi driver. You just used me for a decoy," she raged.

Terry held her protesting hands tight as he whispered below the hubbub of Logan's protestations,

"Never a bit of it, my dear. I loved you the first day you stalled your car in the thick of things on 125th Street, before you even saw me, and I got in the habit of following you around while I was impersonating a taxi driver, to get a chance to know you. Then when I found this—" a wave towards the still-voluble Logan—"had marked you for another one of his prey—well you don't mind if I combined a bit of business with my pleasure?"

Elise's faint "No" was visible, rather than audible.

"It's all right then? Shall it be beefsteak for two?"

"Yes."

"And you won't take back what you promised up there on the Drive?"

"How can I," she laughed, "when my middle name is McBride?"

A Carnival Jangle

There is a merry jangle of bells in the air, an all-pervading sense of jester's noise, and the flaunting vividness of royal colours. The streets swarm with humanity,—humanity in all shapes, manners, forms, laughing, pushing, jostling, crowding, a mass of men and women and children, as varied and assorted in their several individual peculiarities as ever a crowd that gathered in one locality since the days of Babel.

It is Carnival in New Orleans; a brilliant Tuesday in February, when the very air gives forth an ozone intensely exhilarating, making one long to cut capers. The buildings are a blazing mass of royal purple and golden yellow, national flags, bunting, and decorations that laugh in the glint of the Midas sun. The streets are a crush of jesters and maskers, Jim Crows and clowns, ballet girls and Mephistos, Indians and monkeys; of wild and sudden flashes of music, of glittering pageants and comic ones, of befeathered and belled horses; a dream of colour and melody and fantasy gone wild in an effervescent bubble of beauty that shifts and changes and passes kaleidoscope-like before the bewildered eye.

A bevy of bright-eyed girls and boys of that uncertain age that hovers between childhood and maturity, were moving down Canal Street when there was a sudden jostle with another crowd meeting them. For a minute there was a deafening clamour of shouts and laughter, cracking of the whips, which all maskers carry, a jingle and clatter of carnival bells, and the masked and unmasked extricated themselves and moved from each other's paths. But in the confusion a tall Prince of Darkness had whispered to one of the girls in the unmasked crowd: "You'd better come with us, Flo; you're wasting time in that tame gang. Slip off, they'll never miss you; we'll get you a rig, and show you what life is."

And so it happened, when a half-hour passed, and the bright-eyed bevy missed Flo and couldn't find her, wisely giving up the search at last, she, the quietest and most bashful of the lot, was being initiated into the mysteries of "what life is."

Down Bourbon Street and on Toulouse and St. Peter Streets there are quaint little old-world places where one may be disguised effectually for a tiny consideration. Thither, guided by the shapely Mephisto and guarded by the team of jockeys and ballet girls, tripped Flo. Into one of the lowest-ceiled, dingiest, and most ancient-looking of these shops they stepped.

"A disguise for the demoiselle," announced Mephisto to the woman who met them. She was small and wizened and old, with yellow, flabby jaws, a neck like the throat of an alligator, and straight, white hair that stood from her head uncannily stiff.

"But the demoiselle wishes to appear a boy, un petit garçon?" she inquired, gazing eagerly at Flo's long, slender frame. Her voice was old and thin, like the high quavering of an imperfect tuning-fork, and her eyes were sharp as talons in their grasping glance.

"Mademoiselle does not wish such a costume," gruffly responded Mephisto.

"Ma foi, there is no other," said the ancient, shrugging her shoulders. "But one is left now; mademoiselle would make a fine troubadour."

"Flo," said Mephisto, "it's a daredevil scheme, try it; no one will ever know it but us, and we'll die before we tell. Besides, we must; it's late, and you couldn't find your crowd."

And that was why you might have seen a Mephisto and a slender troubadour of lovely form, with mandolin flung across his shoulder, followed by a bevy of jockeys and ballet girls, laughing and singing as they swept down Rampart Street.

When the flash and glare and brilliancy of Canal Street have palled upon the tired eye, when it is yet too soon to go home to such a prosaic thing as dinner, and one still wishes for novelty, then it is wise to go into the lower districts. There is fantasy and fancy and grotesqueness run wild in the costuming and the behaviour of the maskers. Such dances and whoops and leaps as these hideous Indians and devils do indulge in; such wild curvetings and long walks! In the open squares, where whole groups do congregate, it is wonderfully amusing. Then, too, there is a ball in every available hall, a delirious ball, where one may dance all day for ten cents; dance and grow mad for joy, and never know who were your companions, and be yourself unknown. And in the exhilaration of the day, one walks miles and miles, and dances and skips, and the fatigue is never felt.

In Washington Square, away down where Royal Street empties its stream of children great and small into the broad channel of Elysian Fields Avenue, there was a perfect Indian pow-wow. With a little imagination one might have willed away the vision of the surrounding houses, and fancied one's self again in the forest, where the natives were holding a sacred riot. The square was filled with spectators, masked and unmasked. It was amusing to watch these mimic Red-men, they seemed so fierce and earnest.

Suddenly one chief touched another on the elbow. "See that Mephisto and troubadour over there?" he whispered huskily.

"Yes; who are they?"

"I don't know the devil," responded the other, quietly, "but I'd know that other form anywhere. It's Leon, see? I know those white hands like a woman's and that restless head. Ha!"

"But there may be a mistake."

"No. I'd know that one anywhere; I feel it is he. I'll pay him now. Ah, sweetheart, you've waited long, but you shall feast now!" He was caressing something long and lithe and glittering beneath his blanket.

In a masked dance it is easy to give a death-blow between the shoulders. Two crowds meet and laugh and shout and mingle almost inextricably, and if a shriek of pain should arise, it is not noticed in the din, and when they part, if one should stagger and fall bleeding to the ground, can any one tell who has given the blow? There is nothing but an unknown stiletto on the ground, the crowd has dispersed, and masks tell no tales anyway. There is murder, but by whom? for what? *Quien sabe?*

And that is how it happened on Carnival night, in the last mad moments of Rex's reign, a broken-hearted mother sat gazing wide-eyed and mute at a horrible something that lay across the bed. Outside the long sweet march music of many bands floated in as if in mockery, and the flash of rockets and Bengal lights illumined the dead, white face of the girl troubadour.

M'sieu Fortier's Violin

Slowly, one by one, the lights in the French Opera go out, until there is but a single glimmer of pale yellow flickering in the great dark space, a few moments ago all a-glitter with jewels and the radiance of womanhood and a-clash with music. Darkness now, and silence, and a great haunted hush over all, save for the distant cheery voice of a stage hand humming a bar of the opera.

The glimmer of gas makes a halo about the bowed white head of a little old man putting his violin carefully away in its case with aged, trembling, nervous fingers. Old M'sieu Fortier was the last one out every night.

Outside the air was murky, foggy. Gas and electricity were but faint splotches of light on the thick curtain of fog and mist. Around the opera was a mighty bustle of carriages and drivers and footmen, with a car gaining headway in the street now and then, a howling of names and numbers, the laughter and small talk of cloaked society stepping slowly to its carriages, and the more bourgeoisie vocalisation of the foot passengers who streamed along and hummed little bits of music. The fog's denseness was confusing, too, and at one moment it seemed that the little narrow street would become inextricably choked and remain so until some mighty engine would blow the crowd into atoms. It had been a crowded night. From around Toulouse Street, where led the entrance to the troisièmes, from the grand stairway, from the entrance to the quatrièmes, the human stream poured into the street, nearly all with a song on their lips.

M'sieu Fortier stood at the corner, blinking at the beautiful ladies in their carriages. He exchanged a hearty salutation with the saloon-keeper at the corner, then, tenderly carrying his violin case, he trudged down Bourbon Street, a little old, bent, withered figure, with shoulders shrugged up to keep warm, as though the faded brown overcoat were not thick enough.

Down on Bayou Road, not so far from Claiborne Street, was a house, little and old and queer, but quite large enough to hold M'sieu Fortier, a wrinkled dame, and a white cat. He was home but little, for on nearly every day there were rehearsals; then on Tuesday, Thursday, and Saturday nights, and twice Sundays there were performances, so Ma'am Jeanne and the white cat kept house almost always alone. Then, when M'sieu Fortier was at home, why, it was practice, practice all the day, and smoke, snore, sleep at night. Altogether it was not very exhilarating.

M'sieu Fortier had played first violin in the orchestra ever since—well, no one remembered his not playing there. Sometimes there would come breaks in the seasons, and for a year the great building would be dark and silent. Then M'sieu Fortier would do jobs of playing here and there, one night for this ball, another night for that soirée dansante, and in the day, work at his trade,—that of a cigar-maker. But now for seven years there had been no break in the season, and the little old violinist was happy. There is nothing sweeter than a regular job and good music to play, music into which one can put some soul, some expression, and which one must study to understand. Dance music, of the frivolous, frothy kind deemed essential to soirées, is trivial, easy, uninteresting.

So M'sieu Fortier, Ma'am Jeanne, and the white cat lived a peaceful, uneventful existence out on Bayou Road. When the opera season was over in February, M'sieu went back to cigar-making, and the white cat purred none the less contentedly.

It had been a benefit to-night for the leading tenor, and he had chosen "Roland à Ronceveaux," a favourite this season, for his farewell. And, mon Dieu, mused the little M'sieu, but how his voice had rung out bell-like, piercing above the chorus of the first act! Encore after encore was given, and the bravos of the troisièmes were enough to stir the most sluggish of pulses.

"Superbes Pyrenées
Qui dressez dans le ciel,
Vos cimes couronnées
D'un hiver éternelle,
Pour nous livrer passage
Ouvrez vos larges flancs,
Faîtes taire l'orage,
Voici, venir les Francs!"

M'sieu quickened his pace down Bourbon Street as he sang the chorus to himself in a thin old voice, and then, before he could see in the thick fog, he had run into two young men.

"I—I—beg your pardon,—messieurs," he stammered.

"Most certainly," was the careless response; then the speaker, taking a second glance at the object of the rencontre, cried joyfully:

"Oh, M'sieu Fortier, is it you? Why, you are so happy, singing your love sonnet to your lady's eyebrow, that you didn't see a thing but the moon, did you? And who is the fair one who should clog your senses so?"

There was a deprecating shrug from the little man.

"Ma foi, but monsieur must know fo' sho', dat I am too old for love songs!"

"I know nothing save that I want that violin of yours. When is it to be mine, M'sieu Fortier?"

"Nevare, nevare!" exclaimed M'sieu, gripping on as tightly to the case as if he feared it might be wrenched from him. "Me a lovere, and to sell mon violon! Ah, so ver' foolish!"

"Martel," said the first speaker to his companion as they moved on up town, "I wish you knew that little Frenchman. He's a unique specimen. He has the most exquisite violin I've seen in years; beautiful and mellow as a genuine Cremona, and he can make the music leap, sing, laugh, sob, skip, wail, anything you like from under his bow when he wishes. It's something wonderful. We are good friends. Picked him up in my French-town rambles. I've been trying to buy that instrument since—"

"To throw it aside a week later?" lazily inquired Martel. "You are like the rest of these nineteenth-century vandals, you can see nothing picturesque that you do not wish to deface for a souvenir; you cannot even let simple happiness alone, but must needs destroy it in a vain attempt to make it your own or parade it as an advertisement."

As for M'sieu Fortier, he went right on with his song and turned into Bayou Road, his shoulders still shrugged high as though he were cold, and into the quaint little house, where Ma'am Jeanne and the white cat, who always waited up for him at nights, were both nodding over the fire.

It was not long after this that the opera closed, and M'sieu went back to his old out-of-season job. But somehow he did not do as well this spring and summer as always. There is a certain amount of cunning and finesse required to roll a cigar just so, that M'sieu seemed to be losing, whether from age or deterioration it was hard to tell. Nevertheless, there was just about half as much money coming in as formerly, and the quaint little pucker between M'sieu's eyebrows which served for a frown came oftener and stayed longer than ever before.

"Minesse," he said one day to the white cat,—he told all his troubles to her; it was of no use to talk to Ma'am Jeanne, she was too deaf to understand,—"Minesse, we are gettin' po'. You' père git h'old, an' hees han's dey go no mo' rapidement, an' dere be no mo' soirées dese day. Minesse, eef la saison don' hurry up, we shall eat ver' lil' meat."

And Minesse curled her tail and purred.

Before the summer had fairly begun, strange rumours began to float about in musical circles. M. Maugé would no longer manage the opera, but it would be turned into the hands of Americans, a syndicate. Bah! These English-speaking people could do nothing unless there was a trust, a syndicate, a company immense and dishonest. It was going to be a guarantee business, with a strictly financial basis. But worse than all this, the new manager, who was now in France, would not only procure the artists, but a new orchestra, a new leader. M'sieu Fortier grew apprehensive at this, for he knew what the loss of his place would mean to him.

September and October came, and the papers were filled with accounts of the new artists from France and of the new orchestra leader too. He was described as a most talented, progressive, energetic young man. M'sieu Fortier's heart sank at the word "progressive." He was anything but that. The New Orleans Creole blood flowed too sluggishly in his old veins.

November came; the opera reopened. M'sieu Fortier was not re-engaged.

"Minesse," he said with a catch in his voice that strongly resembled a sob, "Minesse, we mus' go hongry sometime. Ah, mon pauvre violon! Ah, mon Dieu, dey put us h'out, an' dey will not have us. Nev' min', we will sing anyhow." And drawing his bow across the strings, he sang in his thin, quavering voice, "Salut demeure, chaste et pure."

It is strange what a peculiar power of fascination former haunts have for the human mind. The criminal, after he has fled from justice, steals back and skulks about the scene of his crime; the employee thrown from work hangs about the place of his former industry; the schoolboy, truant or expelled, peeps in at the school-gate and taunts the good boys within. M'sieu Fortier was no exception. Night after night of the performances he climbed the stairs of the opera and sat, an attentive listener to the orchestra, with one ear inclined to the stage, and a quizzical expression on his wrinkled face. Then he would go home, and pat Minesse, and fondle the violin.

"Ah, Minesse, dose new player! Not one bit can dey play. Such tones, Minesse, such tones! All the time portemento, oh, so ver' bad! Ah, mon chere violon, we can play." And he would play and sing a romance, and smile tenderly to himself.

At first it used to be into the deuxièmes that M'sieu Fortier went, into the front seats. But soon they were too expensive, and after all, one could hear just as well in the fourth row as in the first. After a while even the rear row of the deuxièmes was too costly, and the little musician wended his way with the plebeians around on Toulouse Street, and climbed the long, tedious flight of stairs into the troisièmes. It makes no difference to be one row higher. It was more to the liking, after all. One felt more at home up here among the people. If one was thirsty, one could drink a glass of wine or beer being passed about by the libretto boys, and the music sounded just as well.

But it happened one night that M'sieu could not even afford to climb the Toulouse Street stairs. To be sure, there was yet another gallery, the quatrièmes, where the peanut boys went for a dime, but M'sieu could not get down to that yet. So he stayed outside until all the beautiful women in their warm wraps, a bright-hued chattering throng, came down the grand staircase to their carriages.

It was on one of these nights that Courcey and Martel found him shivering at the corner.

"Hello, M'sieu Fortier," cried Courcey, "are you ready to let me have that violin yet?"

"For shame!" interrupted Martel.

"Fifty dollars, you know," continued Courcey, taking no heed of his friend's interpolation.

M'sieu Fortier made a courtly bow. "Eef Monsieur will call at my 'ouse on de morrow, he may have mon violon," he said huskily; then turned abruptly on his heel, and went down Bourbon Street, his shoulders drawn high as though he were cold.

When Courcey and Martel entered the gate of the little house on Bayou Road the next day, there floated out to their ears a wordless song thrilling from the violin, a song that told more than speech or tears or gestures could have done of the utter sorrow and desolation of the little old man. They walked softly up the short red brick walk and tapped at the door. Within, M'sieu Fortier was caressing the violin, with silent tears streaming down his wrinkled gray face.

There was not much said on either side. Courcey came away with the instrument, leaving the money behind, while Martel grumbled at the essentially sordid, mercenary spirit of the world. M'sieu Fortier turned back into the room, after bowing his visitors out with old-time French courtliness, and turning to the sleepy white cat, said with a dry sob:

"Minesse, dere's only me an' you now."

About six days later, Courcey's morning dreams were disturbed by the announcement of a visitor. Hastily doing a toilet, he descended the stairs to find M'sieu Fortier nervously pacing the hall floor.

"I come fo' bring back you' money, yaas. I cannot sleep, I cannot eat, I only cry, and t'ink, and weesh fo' mon violon; and Minesse, an' de ol' woman too, dey mope an' look bad too, all for mon violon. I try fo' to use dat money, but eet burn an' sting lak blood money. I feel lak' I done sol' my child. I cannot go at l'opera no mo', I t'ink of mon violon. I starve befo' I live widout. My heart, he is broke, I die for mon violon."

Courcey left the room and returned with the instrument.

"M'sieu Fortier," he said, bowing low, as he handed the case to the little man, "take your violin; it was a whim with me, a passion with you. And as for the money, why, keep that too; it was worth a hundred dollars to have possessed such an instrument even for six days."

Sister Josepha

Sister Josepha told her beads mechanically, her fingers numb with the accustomed exercise. The little organ creaked a dismal "O Salutaris," and she still knelt on the floor, her white-bonneted head nodding suspiciously. The Mother Superior gave a sharp glance at the tired figure; then, as a sudden lurch forward brought the little sister back to consciousness, Mother's eyes relaxed into a genuine smile.

The bell tolled the end of vespers, and the sombre-robed nuns filed out of the chapel to go about their evening duties. Little Sister Josepha's work was to attend to the household lamps, but there must have been as much oil spilled upon the table to-night as was put in the vessels. The small brown hands trembled so that most of the wicks were trimmed with points at one corner which caused them to smoke that night.

"Oh, cher Seigneur," she sighed, giving an impatient polish to a refractory chimney, "it is wicked and sinful, I know, but I am so tired. I can't be happy and sing any more. It doesn't seem right for le bon Dieu to have me all cooped up here with nothing to see but stray visitors, and always the same old work, teaching those mean little girls to sew, and washing and filling the same old lamps. Pah!" And she polished the chimney with a sudden vigorous jerk which threatened destruction.

They were rebellious prayers that the red mouth murmured that night, and a restless figure that tossed on the hard dormitory bed. Sister Dominica called from her couch to know if Sister Josepha were ill.

"No," was the somewhat short response; then a muttered, "Why can't they let me alone for a minute? That pale-eyed Sister Dominica never sleeps; that's why she is so ugly."

About fifteen years before this night some one had brought to the orphan asylum connected with this convent, du Sacré Cœur, a round, dimpled bit of three-year-old humanity, who regarded the world from a pair of gravely twinkling black eyes, and only took a chubby thumb out of a rosy mouth long enough to answer in monosyllabic French. It was a child without an identity; there was but one name that any one seemed to know, and that, too, was vague,—Camille.

She grew up with the rest of the waifs; scraps of French and American civilization thrown together to develop a seemingly inconsistent miniature world. Mademoiselle Camille was a queen among them, a pretty little tyrant who ruled the children and dominated the more timid sisters in charge.

One day an awakening came. When she was fifteen, and almost fully ripened into a glorious tropical beauty of the type that matures early, some visitors to the convent were fascinated by her and asked the Mother Superior to give the girl into their keeping.

Camille fled like a frightened fawn into the yard, and

was only unearthed with some difficulty from behind a group of palms. Sulky and pouting, she was led into the parlour, picking at her blue pinafore like a spoiled infant.

"The lady and gentleman wish you to go home with them, Camille," said the Mother Superior, in the language of the convent. Her voice was kind and gentle apparently; but the child, accustomed to its various inflections, detected a steely ring behind its softness, like the proverbial iron hand in the velvet glove.

"You must understand, madame," continued Mother, in stilted English, "that we never force children from us. We are ever glad to place them in comfortable—how you say that?—quarters—maisons—homes—bien! But we will not make them go if they do not wish."

Camille stole a glance at her would-be guardians, and decided instantly, impulsively, finally. The woman suited her; but the man! It was doubtless intuition of the quick, vivacious sort which belonged to her blood that served her. Untutored in worldly knowledge, she could not divine the meaning of the pronounced leers and admiration of her physical charms which gleamed in the man's face, but she knew it made her feel creepy, and stoutly refused to go.

Next day Camille was summoned from a task to the Mother Superior's parlour. The other girls gazed with envy upon her as she dashed down the courtyard with impetuous movement. Camille, they decided crossly, received too much notice. It was Camille this, Camille that; she was pretty, it was to be expected. Even Father Ray lingered longer in his blessing when his hands pressed her silky black hair.

As she entered the parlour, a strange chill swept over the girl. The room was not an unaccustomed one, for she had swept it many times, but to-day the stiff black chairs, the dismal crucifixes, the gleaming whiteness of the walls, even the cheap lithograph of the Madonna which Camille had always regarded as a perfect specimen of art, seemed cold and mean.

"Camille, ma chère," said Mother, "I am extremely displeased with you. Why did you not wish to go with Monsieur and Madame Lafayé yesterday?"

The girl uncrossed her hands from her bosom, and spread them out in a deprecating gesture.

"Mais, ma mère, I was afraid."

Mother's face grew stern. "No foolishness now," she exclaimed.

"It is not foolishness, ma mère; I could not help it, but that man looked at me so funny, I felt all cold chills down my back. Oh, dear Mother, I love the convent and the sisters so, I just want to stay and be a sister too, may I?"

And thus it was that Camille took the white veil at sixteen years. Now that the period of novitiate was over, it was just beginning to dawn upon her that she had made a mistake.

"Maybe it would have been better had I gone with the funny-looking lady and gentleman," she mused bitterly one night. "Oh, Seigneur, I'm so tired and impatient; it's so dull here, and, dear God, I'm so young."

There was no help for it. One must arise in the morning, and help in the refectory with the stupid Sister Francesca, and go about one's duties with a prayerful mien, and not even let a sigh escape when one's head ached with the eternal telling of beads.

A great fête day was coming, and an atmosphere of preparation and mild excitement pervaded the brown walls of the convent like a delicate aroma. The old Cathedral around the corner had stood a hundred years, and all the city was rising to do honour to its age and time-softened beauty. There would be a service, oh, but such a one! with two Cardinals, and Archbishops and Bishops, and all the accompanying glitter of soldiers and orchestras. The little sisters of the Convent du Sacré Cœur clasped their hands in anticipation of the holy joy. Sister Josepha curled her lip, she was so tired of churchly pleasures.

The day came, a gold and blue spring day, when the air hung heavy with the scent of roses and magnolias, and the sunbeams fairly laughed as they kissed the houses. The old Cathedral stood gray and solemn, and the flowers in Jackson Square smiled cheery birthday greetings across the way. The crowd around the door surged and pressed and pushed in its eagerness to get within. Ribbons stretched across the banquette were of no avail to repress it, and important ushers with cardinal colours could do little more.

The Sacred Heart sisters filed slowly in at the side door, creating a momentary flutter as they paced reverently to their seats, guarding the blue-bonneted orphans. Sister Josepha, determined to see as much of the world as she could, kept her big black eyes opened wide, as the church rapidly filled with the fashionably dressed, perfumed, rustling, and self-conscious throng.

Her heart beat quickly. The rebellious thoughts that will arise in the most philosophical of us surged in her small heavily gowned bosom. For her were the gray things, the neutral tinted skies, the ugly garb, the coarse meats; for them the rainbow, the ethereal airiness of earthly joys, the bonbons and glacés of the world. Sister Josepha did not know that the rainbow is elusive, and its colours but the illumination of tears; she had never been told that earthly ethereality is necessarily ephemeral, nor that bonbons and glacés, whether of the palate or of the soul, nauseate and pall upon the taste. Dear God, forgive her, for she bent with contrite tears over her worn rosary, and glanced no more at the worldly glitter of femininity.

The sunbeams streamed through the high windows in purple and crimson lights upon a veritable fugue of colour. Within the seats, crush upon crush of spring millinery; within the aisles erect lines of gold-braided, gold-buttoned military. Upon the altar, broad sweeps of golden robes, great dashes of crimson skirts, mitres and gleaming crosses, the soft neutral hue of rich lace vestments; the tender heads of childhood in picturesque attire; the proud, golden magnificence of the domed altar with its weighting mass of lilies and wide-eyed roses, and the long candles that sparkled their yellow star points above the reverent throng within the altar rails.

The soft baritone of the Cardinal intoned a single phrase in the suspended silence. The censer took up the note in its delicate clink clink, as it swung to and fro in the hands of a fair-haired child. Then the organ, pausing an instant in a deep, mellow, long-drawn note, burst suddenly into a magnificent strain, and the choir sang forth, "Kyrie Eleïson, Christe Eleïson." One voice, flute-like, piercing, sweet, rang high over the rest. Sister Josepha heard and trembled, as she buried her face in her hands, and let her tears fall, like other beads, through her rosary.

It was when the final word of the service had been intoned, the last peal of the exit march had died away, that she looked up meekly, to encounter a pair of youthful brown eyes gazing pityingly upon her. That was all she remembered for a moment, that the eyes were youthful and handsome and tender. Later, she saw that they were placed in a rather beautiful boyish face, surmounted by waves of brown hair, curling and soft, and that the head was set on a pair of shoulders decked in military uniform. Then the brown eyes marched away with the rest of the rear guard, and the white-bonneted sisters filed out the side door, through the narrow court, back into the brown convent.

That night Sister Josepha tossed more than usual on her hard bed, and clasped her fingers often in prayer to quell the wickedness in her heart. Turn where she would, pray as she might, there was ever a pair of tender, pitying brown eyes, haunting her persistently. The squeaky organ at vespers intoned the clank of military accoutrements to her ears, the white bonnets of the sisters about her faded into mists of curling brown hair. Briefly, Sister Josepha was in love.

The days went on pretty much as before, save for the one little heart that beat rebelliously now and then, though it tried so hard to be submissive. There was the morning work in the refectory, the stupid little girls to teach sewing, and the insatiable lamps that were so greedy for oil. And always the tender, boyish brown eyes, that looked so sorrowfully at the fragile, beautiful little sister, haunting, following, pleading.

Perchance, had Sister Josepha been in the world, the eyes would have been an incident. But in this home of self-repression and retrospection, it was a life-story. The eyes had gone their way, doubtless forgetting the little sister they pitied; but the little sister?

The days glided into weeks, the weeks into months. Thoughts of escape had come to Sister Josepha, to flee into the world, to merge in the great city where recognition was impossible, and, working her way like the rest of humanity, perchance encounter the eyes again.

It was all planned and ready. She would wait until some morning when the little band of black-robed sisters wended their way to mass at the Cathedral. When it was time to file out the side-door into the courtway, she would linger at prayers, then slip out another door, and unseen glide up Chartres Street to Canal, and once there, mingle in the throng that filled the wide thoroughfare. Beyond this first plan she could think no further. Penniless, garbed, and shaven though she would be, other difficulties never presented themselves to her. She would rely on the mercies of the world to help her escape from this torturing life of inertia. It seemed easy now that the first step of decision had been taken.

The Saturday night before the final day had come, and she lay feverishly nervous in her narrow little bed, wondering with wide-eyed fear at the morrow. Pale-eyed

Sister Dominica and Sister Francesca were whispering together in the dark silence, and Sister Josepha's ears pricked up as she heard her name.

"She is not well, poor child," said Francesca. "I fear the life is too confining."

"It is best for her," was the reply. "You know, sister, how hard it would be for her in the world, with no name but Camille, no friends, and her beauty; and then—"

Sister Josepha heard no more, for her heart beating tumultuously in her bosom drowned the rest. Like the rush of the bitter salt tide over a drowning man clinging to a spar, came the complete submerging of her hopes of another life. No name but Camille, that was true; no nationality, for she could never tell from whom or whence she came; no friends, and a beauty that not even an ungainly bonnet and shaven head could hide. In a flash she realised the deception of the life she would lead, and the cruel self-torture of wonder at her own identity. Already, as if in anticipation of the world's questionings, she was asking herself, "Who am I? What am I?"

The next morning the sisters du Sacré Cœur filed into the Cathedral at High Mass, and bent devout knees at the general confession. "Confiteor Deo omnipotenti," murmured the priest; and tremblingly one little sister followed the words, "Je confesse à Dieu, tout puissant—que j'ai beaucoup péché par pensées—c'est ma faute—c'est ma faute—c'est ma très grande faute."

The organ pealed forth as mass ended, the throng slowly filed out, and the sisters paced through the courtway back into the brown convent walls. One paused at the entrance, and gazed with swift longing eyes in the direction of narrow, squalid Chartres Street, then, with a gulping sob, followed the rest, and vanished behind the heavy door.

His Great Career

The travel-scarred motorcar came to a pause in the driveway of the great mountain mansion. "The Squire," as he was lovingly called for miles around, greeted the owner of the car as he rather stiffly set foot on the ground.

"It's good of you to come up here to see us in our mountain fastness," he said warmly.

"Didn't know you lived here until we broke down somewhere in your peaks and crags, and Martin inquired of the nearest civilized house."

The Squire talked cheerfully as he carried the bags of the great criminal lawyer up the broad walk.

"We're having a big house party here," he explained to the group of guests on the veranda. "My wife's birthday, and when we give a party up here, it means a weekend stay, for we have to go so far for our festivities, it would be a pity to go right home."

The great lawyer was introduced to the fluttering and flattered group of maidens and wives, and to the hearty men who hovered on the edges. He bent his great grizzled frame over small eager hands, while his host stood by, enjoying his embarrassment in the pause before he went to his room.

"And so you're married?" asked the lawyer, as they went up the broad stairs.

"Fifteen years. You remember when my health broke eighteen years ago? I found *her* here in a sanitarium, wrecked too, and 'sick of that disease called life.' Between us, we mended our lives, and then she didn't care for the east and all that it means any more than I did—so we stayed, and here we are."

The great lawyer revelled in the scene, a marvelous panorama spreading out from the window.

"Prominent citizen, leader of the community, and the rest?" he asked smilingly.

The Squire was modest. "Well, we've helped build the community, and all that sort of thing. You can't live in a place without being part of it. And you, old Hard-head, you've become one of the most famous lawyers in the country!"

The lawyer waved a deprecating hand. "I'm motoring in out of the way places now to forget it awhile."

The veranda was not in a mood to allow him to forget. Famous celebrities did not drop into their lives often enough for them to be blasé. The lawyer put down the excellent cocktail that his host brought him in lieu of tea, and inquired for the mistress of the house. She had ridden to town for a last bit of foolery for tonight's costume party, explained the Squire.

The almond-eyed widow was subtly intent on opening up a flood of reminiscences. She fluttered slender hands and widened black eyes suggestively. Even the great lawyer's habitual taciturnity relaxed under the enveloping warmth of remembering the night she had sworn to be avenged on the slim, pale woman, who had taken him, her legitimate prey. A wife and a widow since, but the almond eyes still avid for vengeance.

"You must have had some interesting experiences, have you not? Oh, do tell us about some of your early struggles."

The great lawyer expanded under the enveloping perfume of her incense.

"Well," he began, his great voice booming softly in the mountain sunlight, "I shall never forget my first case. I was a briefless barrister, and hungry, or I would not have taken it. Everyone concerned in the affair is dead now, so I can smile at it. My first client was a murderer, a woman. She confessed the truth to me, and expected me to clear her."

"And did you?" chorused an octave of soprano voices.

"Yes. It was the beginning of my career."

A soft intake of breath from the widow, and a flattering flutter from the rest of the veranda left the great lawyer to turn to his host.

But the Squire was oblivious, for coming up the walk was the mistress of the mansion. His soul was in his eyes as he watched her. Her eyes glowed, and her face was wind-whipped from riding; she had taken off her hat and her packages dangled from her arm. The lawyer stood in intent stillness. The same lithe form. The same aureole of auburn hair, as yet untinged by gray. The same still, quiet little face with deep pools of eyes. The same questioning droop of head. She came quickly up the walk and onto the veranda with incredible lightness.

"My dear," said the Squire, his voice a protecting caress, "this is—"

But she extended her hand smilingly to the great lawyer, grasping his with welcoming warmth.

"I did not die, you see," she said in her deep, vibrant voice, "The west gave me health and happiness," and still holding his hand with proprietary grasp, she turned to the group on the veranda.

"Mr. Booth is an old friend of mine, too. You see, I was his very first client, and I flatter myself that I started him on his great career."

Little Miss Sophie

When Miss Sophie knew consciousness again, the long, faint, swelling notes of the organ were dying away in distant echoes through the great arches of the silent church, and she was alone, crouching in a little, forsaken black heap at the altar of the Virgin. The twinkling tapers shone pityingly upon her, the beneficent smile of the white-robed Madonna seemed to whisper comfort. A long gust of chill air swept up the aisles, and Miss Sophie shivered not from cold, but from nervousness.

But darkness was falling, and soon the lights would be lowered, and the great massive doors would be closed; so, gathering her thin little cape about her frail shoulders, Miss Sophie hurried out, and along the brilliant noisy streets home.

It was a wretched, lonely little room, where the cracks let the boisterous wind whistle through, and the smoky, grimy walls looked cheerless and unhomelike. A miserable little room in a miserable little cottage in one of the squalid streets of the Third District that nature and the city fathers seemed to have forgotten.

As bare and comfortless as the room was Miss Sophie's life. She rented these four walls from an unkempt little Creole woman, whose progeny seemed like the promised offspring of Abraham. She scarcely kept the flickering life in her pale little body by the unceasing toil of a pair of bony hands, stitching, stitching, ceaselessly, wearingly, on the bands and pockets of trousers. It was her bread, this monotonous, unending work; and though whole days and nights constant labour brought but the most meagre recompense, it was her only hope of life.

She sat before the little charcoal brazier and warmed her transparent, needle-pricked fingers, thinking meanwhile of the strange events of the day. She had been up town to carry the great, black bundle of coarse pants and vests to the factory and to receive her small pittance, and on the way home stopped in at the Jesuit Church to say her little prayer at the altar of the calm white Virgin. There had been a wondrous burst of music from the great organ as she knelt there, an overpowering perfume of many flowers, the glittering dazzle of many lights, and the dainty frou-frou made by the silken skirts of wedding guests. So Miss Sophie stayed to the wedding; for what feminine heart, be it ever so old and seared, does not delight in one? And why should not a poor little Creole old maid be interested too?

Then the wedding party had filed in solemnly, to the rolling, swelling tones of the organ. Important-looking groomsmen; dainty, fluffy, white-robed maids; stately, satin-robed, illusion-veiled bride, and happy groom. She leaned forward to catch a better glimpse of their faces. "Ah!"—

Those near the Virgin's altar who heard a faint sigh and rustle on the steps glanced curiously as they saw a slight black-robed figure clutch the railing and lean her head against it. Miss Sophie had fainted.

"I must have been hungry," she mused over the charcoal fire in her little room, "I must have been hungry;" and she smiled a wan smile, and busied herself getting her evening meal of coffee and bread and ham.

If one were given to pity, the first thought that would rush to one's lips at sight of Miss Sophie would have been, "Poor little woman!" She had come among the bareness and sordidness of this neighbourhood five years ago, robed in crape, and crying with great sobs that seemed to shake the vitality out of her. Perfectly silent, too, she was about her former life; but for all that, Michel, the quartee grocer at the corner, and Madame Laurent, who kept the rabbé shop opposite, had fixed it all up between them, of her sad history and past glories. Not that they knew; but then Michel must invent something when the neighbours came to him as their fountain-head of wisdom.

One morning little Miss Sophie opened wide her dingy windows to catch the early freshness of the autumn wind as it whistled through the yellow-leafed trees. It was one of those calm, blue-misted, balmy, November days that New Orleans can have when all the rest of the country is fur-wrapped. Miss Sophie pulled her machine to the window, where the sweet, damp wind could whisk among her black locks.

Whirr, whirr, went the machine, ticking fast and lightly over the belts of the rough jeans pants. Whirr, whirr, yes, and Miss Sophie was actually humming a tune! She felt strangely light to-day.

"Ma foi," muttered Michel, strolling across the street to where Madame Laurent sat sewing behind the counter on blue and brown-checked aprons, "but the little ma'amselle sings. Perhaps she recollects."

"Perhaps," muttered the rabbé woman.

But little Miss Sophie felt restless. A strange impulse seemed drawing her up town, and the machine seemed to run slow, slow, before it would stitch all of the endless number of jeans belts. Her fingers trembled with nervous haste as she pinned up the unwieldy black bundle of finished work, and her feet fairly tripped over each other in their eagerness to get to Claiborne Street, where she could board the up-town car. There was a feverish desire to go somewhere, a sense of elation, a foolish happiness that brought a faint echo of colour into her pinched cheeks. She wondered why.

No one noticed her in the car. Passengers on the Claiborne line are too much accustomed to frail little black-robed women with big, black bundles; it is one of the city's most pitiful sights. She leaned her head out of the window to catch a glimpse of the oleanders on Bayou Road, when her attention was caught by a conversation in the car.

"Yes, it's too bad for Neale, and lately married too," said the elder man. "I can't see what he is to do."

Neale! She pricked up her ears. That was the name of the groom in the Jesuit Church.

"How did it happen?" languidly inquired the younger. He was a stranger, evidently; a stranger with a high regard for the faultlessness of male attire.

"Well, the firm failed first; he didn't mind that much,

he was so sure of his uncle's inheritance repairing his lost fortunes; but suddenly this difficulty of identification springs up, and he is literally on the verge of ruin."

"Won't some of you fellows who've known him all your lives do to identify him?"

"Gracious man, we've tried; but the absurd old will expressly stipulates that he shall be known only by a certain quaint Roman ring, and unless he has it, no identification, no fortune. He has given the ring away, and that settles it."

"Well, you're all chumps. Why doesn't he get the ring from the owner?"

"Easily said; but—it seems that Neale had some little Creole love-affair some years ago, and gave this ring to his dusky-eyed fiancée. You know how Neale is with his love-affairs, went off and forgot the girl in a month. It seems, however, she took it to heart,—so much so that he's ashamed to try to find her or the ring."

Miss Sophie heard no more as she gazed out into the dusty grass. There were tears in her eyes, hot blinding ones that wouldn't drop for pride, but stayed and scalded. She knew the story, with all its embellishment of heartaches. She knew the ring, too. She remembered the day she had kissed and wept and fondled it, until it seemed her heart must burst under its load of grief before she took it to the pawn-broker's that another might be eased before the end came,—that other her father. The little "Creole love affair" of Neale's had not always been poor and old and jaded-looking; but reverses must come, even Neale knew that, so the ring was at the Mont de Piété. Still he must have it, it was his; it would save him from disgrace and suffering and from bringing the white-gowned bride into sorrow. He must have it; but how?

There it was still at the pawn-broker's; no one would have such an odd jewel, and the ticket was home in the bureau drawer. Well, he must have it; she might starve in the attempt. Such a thing as going to him and telling him that he might redeem it was an impossibility. That good, straight-backed, stiff-necked Creole blood would have risen in all its strength and choked her. No; as a present had the quaint Roman circlet been placed upon her finger, as a present should it be returned.

The bumping car rode slowly, and the hot thoughts beat heavily in her poor little head. He must have the ring; but how—the ring—the Roman ring—the white-robed bride starving—she was going mad—ah yes—the church.

There it was, right in the busiest, most bustling part of the town, its fresco and bronze and iron quaintly suggestive of mediaeval times. Within, all was cool and dim and restful, with the faintest whiff of lingering incense rising and pervading the gray arches. Yes, the Virgin would know and have pity; the sweet, white-robed Virgin at the pretty flower-decked altar, or the one away up in the niche, far above the golden dome where the Host was.

Titiche, the busybody of the house, noticed that Miss Sophie's bundle was larger than usual that afternoon. "Ah, poor woman!" sighed Titiche's mother, "she would be rich for Christmas."

The bundle grew larger each day, and Miss Sophie

grew smaller. The damp, cold rain and mist closed the white-curtained window, but always there behind the sewing-machine drooped and bobbed the little black-robed figure. Whirr, whirr went the wheels, and the coarse jeans pants piled in great heaps at her side. The Claiborne Street car saw her oftener than before, and the sweet white Virgin in the flowered niche above the gold-domed altar smiled at the little supplicant almost every day.

"Ma foi," said the slatternly landlady to Madame Laurent and Michel one day, "I no see how she live! Eat? Nothin', nothin', almos', and las' night when it was so cold and foggy, eh? I hav' to mek him build fire. She mos' freeze."

Whereupon the rumour spread that Miss Sophie was starving herself to death to get some luckless relative out of jail for Christmas; a rumour which enveloped her scraggy little figure with a kind of halo to the neighbours when she appeared on the streets.

November had merged into December, and the little pile of coins was yet far from the sum needed. Dear God! how the money did have to go! The rent and the groceries and the coal, though, to be sure, she used a precious bit of that. Would all the work and saving and skimping do good? Maybe, yes, maybe by Christmas.

Christmas Eve on Royal Street is no place for a weakling, for the shouts and carousals of the roisterers will strike fear into the bravest ones. Yet amid the cries and yells, the deafening blow of horns and tin whistles, and the really dangerous fusillade of fireworks, a little figure hurried along, one hand clutching tightly the battered hat that the rude merry-makers had torn off, the other grasping under the thin black cape a worn little pocketbook.

Into the Mont de Piété she ran breathless, eager. The ticket? Here, worn, crumpled. The ring? It was not gone? No, thank Heaven! It was a joy well worth her toil, she thought, to have it again.

Had Titiche not been shooting crackers on the banquette instead of peering into the crack, as was his wont, his big, round black eyes would have grown saucer-wide to see little Miss Sophie kiss and fondle a ring, an ugly clumsy band of gold.

"Ah, dear ring," she murmured, "once you were his, and you shall be his again. You shall be on his finger, and perhaps touch his heart. Dear ring, ma chère petite de ma cœur, chérie de ma cœur. Je t'aime, je t'aime, oui, oui. You are his; you were mine once too. To-night, just one night, I'll keep you—then—to-morrow, you shall go where you can save him."

The loud whistles and horns of the little ones rose on the balmy air next morning. No one would doubt it was Christmas Day, even if doors and windows were open wide to let in cool air. Why, there was Christmas even in the very look of the mules on the poky cars; there was Christmas noise in the streets, and Christmas toys and Christmas odours, savoury ones that made the nose wrinkle approvingly, issuing from the kitchen. Michel and Madame Laurent smiled greetings across the street at each other, and the salutation from a passer-by recalled the many-progenied landlady to herself.

"Miss Sophie, well, po' soul, not ver' much Chris'mas

for her. Mais, I'll jus' call him in fo' to spen' the day with me. Eet'll cheer her a bit."

It was so clean and orderly within the poor little room. Not a speck of dust or a litter of any kind on the quaint little old-time high bureau, unless you might except a sheet of paper lying loose with something written on it. Titiche had evidently inherited his prying propensities, for the landlady turned it over and read,—

> *LOUIS,—Here is the ring. I return it to you. I heard you needed it. I hope it comes not too late.*
> *SOPHIE.*

"The ring, where?" muttered the landlady. There it was, clasped between her fingers on her bosom,—a bosom white and cold, under a cold happy face. Christmas had indeed dawned for Miss Sophie.

Odalie

Now and then Carnival time comes at the time of the good Saint Valentine, and then sometimes it comes as late as the warm days in March, when spring is indeed upon us, and the greenness of the grass outvies the green in the royal standards.

Days and days before the Carnival proper, New Orleans begins to take on a festive appearance. Here and there the royal flags with their glowing greens and violets and yellows appear, and then, as if by magic, the streets and buildings flame and burst like poppies out of bud, into a glorious refulgence of colour that steeps the senses into a languorous acceptance of warmth and beauty.

On Mardi Gras day, as you know, it is a town gone mad with folly. A huge masked ball emptied into the streets at daylight; a meeting of all nations on common ground, a pot-pourri of every conceivable human ingredient, but faintly describes it all. There are music and flowers, cries and laughter and song and joyousness, and never an aching heart to show its sorrow or dim the happiness of the streets. A wondrous thing, this Carnival!

But the old cronies down in Frenchtown, who know everything, and can recite you many a story, tell of one sad heart on Mardi Gras years ago. It was a woman's, of course; for "Il est toujours les femmes qui sont malheureuses," says an old proverb, and perhaps it is right. This woman—a child, she would be called elsewhere, save in this land of tropical growth and precocity—lost her heart to one who never knew, a very common story, by the way, but one which would have been quite distasteful to the haughty judge, her father, had he known.

Odalie was beautiful. Odalie was haughty too, but gracious enough to those who pleased her dainty fancy. In the old French house on Royal Street, with its quaint windows and Spanish courtyard green and cool, and made musical by the plashing of the fountain and the trill of caged birds, lived Odalie in convent-like seclusion. Monsieur le Juge was determined no hawk should break through the cage and steal his dove; and so, though there was no mother, a stern duenna aunt kept faithful watch.

Alas for the precautions of la Tante! Bright eyes that search for other bright eyes in which lurks the spirit of youth and mischief are ever on the look-out, even in church. Dutifully was Odalie marched to the Cathedral every Sunday to mass, and Tante Louise, nodding devoutly over her beads, could not see the blushes and glances full of meaning, a whole code of signals as it were, that passed between Odalie and Pierre, the impecunious young clerk in the courtroom.

Odalie loved, perhaps, because there was not much else to do. When one is shut up in a great French house with a grim sleepy tante and no companions of one's own age, life becomes a dull thing, and one is ready for any new sensation, particularly if in the veins there bounds the tempestuous Spanish-French blood that Monsieur le Juge boasted of. So Odalie hugged the image of her Pierre during the week days, and played tremulous little love-songs to it in the twilight when la Tante dozed over her devotion book, and on Sundays at mass there were glances and blushes, and mayhap, at some especially remembered time, the touch of finger-tips at the holy-water font, while la Tante dropped her last genuflexion.

Then came the Carnival time, and one little heart beat faster, as the gray house on Royal Street hung out its many-hued flags, and draped its grim front with glowing colours. It was to be a time of joy and relaxation, when every one could go abroad, and in the crowds one could speak to whom one chose. Unconscious plans formulated, and the petite Odalie was quite happy as the time drew near.

"Only think, Tante Louise," she would cry, "what a happy time it is to be!"

But Tante Louise only grumbled, as was her wont.

It was Mardi Gras day at last, and early through her window Odalie could hear the jingle of folly bells on the maskers' costumes, the tinkle of music, and the echoing strains of songs. Up to her ears there floated the laughter of the older maskers, and the screams of the little children frightened at their own images under the mask and domino. What a hurry to be out and in the motley merry throng, to be pacing Royal Street to Canal Street, where was life and the world!

They were tired eyes with which Odalie looked at

the gay pageant at last, tired with watching throng after throng of maskers, of the unmasked, of peering into the cartsful of singing minstrels, into carriages of revellers, hoping for a glimpse of Pierre the devout. The allegorical carts rumbling by with their important red-clothed horses were beginning to lose charm, the disguises showed tawdry, even the gay-hued flags fluttered sadly to Odalie. Mardi Gras was a tiresome day, after all, she sighed, and Tante Louise agreed with her for once.

Six o'clock had come, the hour when all masks must be removed. The long red rays of the setting sun glinted athwart the many-hued costumes of the revellers trooping unmasked homeward to rest for the night's last mad frolic.

Down Toulouse Street there came the merriest throng of all. Young men and women in dainty, fairy-like garb, dancers, and dresses of the picturesque Empire, a butterfly or two and a dame here and there with powdered hair and graces of olden time. Singing with unmasked faces, they danced toward Tante Louise and Odalie. She stood with eyes lustrous and tear-heavy, for there in the front was Pierre, Pierre the faithless, his arms about the slender waist of a butterfly, whose tinselled powdered hair floated across the lace ruffles of his Empire coat.

"Pierre!" cried Odalie, softly. No one heard, for it was a mere faint breath and fell unheeded. Instead the laughing throng pelted her with flowers and candy and went their way, and even Pierre did not see.

You see, when one is shut up in the grim walls of a Royal Street house, with no one but a Tante Louise and a grim judge, how is one to learn that in this world there are faithless ones who may glance tenderly into one's eyes at mass and pass the holy water on caressing fingers without being madly in love? There was no one to tell Odalie, so she sat at home in the dull first days of Lent, and nursed her dear dead love, and mourned as women have done from time immemorial over the faithlessness of man. And when one day she asked that she might go back to the Ursulines' convent where her childish days were spent, only to go this time as a nun, Monsieur le Juge and Tante Louise thought it quite the proper and convenient thing to do; for how were they to know the secret of that Mardi Gras day?

The Goodness of St. Rocque

Manuela was tall and slender and graceful, and once you knew her the lithe form could never be mistaken. She walked with the easy spring that comes from a perfectly arched foot. To-day she swept swiftly down Marais Street, casting a quick glance here and there from under her heavy veil as if she feared she was being followed. If you had peered under the veil, you would have seen that Manuela's dark eyes were swollen and discoloured about the lids, as though they had known a sleepless, tearful night.

There had been a picnic the day before, and as merry a crowd of giddy, chattering Creole girls and boys as ever you could see boarded the ramshackle dummy-train that puffed its way wheezily out wide Elysian Fields Street, around the lily-covered bayous, to Milneburg-on-the-Lake. Now, a picnic at Milneburg is a thing to be remembered for ever. One charters a rickety-looking, weather-beaten dancing-pavilion, built over the water, and after storing the children—for your true Creole never leaves the small folks at home—and the baskets and mothers downstairs, the young folks go upstairs and dance to the tune of the best band you ever heard. For what can equal the music of a violin, a guitar, a cornet, and a bass viol to trip the quadrille to at a picnic?

Then one can fish in the lake and go bathing under the prim bath-houses, so severely separated sexually, and go rowing on the lake in a trim boat, followed by the shrill warnings of anxious mamans. And in the evening one comes home, hat crowned with cool gray Spanish moss, hands burdened with fantastic latanier baskets woven by the brown bayou boys, hand in hand with your dearest one, tired but happy.

At this particular picnic, however, there had been bitterness of spirit. Theophilé was Manuela's own especial property, and Theophilé had proven false. He had not danced a single waltz or quadrille with Manuela, but had deserted her for Claralie, blonde and petite. It was Claralie whom Theophilé had rowed out on the lake; it was Claralie whom Theophilé had gallantly led to dinner; it was Claralie's hat that he wreathed with Spanish moss, and Claralie whom he escorted home after the jolly singing ride in town on the little dummy-train.

Not that Manuela lacked partners or admirers. Dear no! she was too graceful and beautiful for that. There had been more than enough for her. But Manuela loved Theophilé, you see, and no one could take his place. Still, she had tossed her head and let her silvery laughter ring out in the dance, as though she were the happiest of mortals, and had tripped home with Henri, leaning on his arm, and looking up into his eyes as though she adored him.

This morning she showed the traces of a sleepless night and an aching heart as she walked down Marais Street. Across wide St. Rocque Avenue she hastened. "Two blocks to the river and one below—" she repeated to herself breathlessly. Then she stood on the corner gazing about her, until with a final summoning of a desperate courage she dived through a small wicket gate into a garden of weed-choked flowers.

There was a hoarse, rusty little bell on the gate that gave querulous tongue as she pushed it open. The house that sat back in the yard was little and old and weather-beaten. Its one-story frame had once been painted, but that was a memory remote and traditional. A straggling morning-glory strove to conceal its time-ravaged face. The little walk of broken bits of brick was reddened carefully, and the one little step was scrupulously yellow-washed, which denoted that the occupants were cleanly as well as religious.

Manuela's timid knock was answered by a harsh "Entrez."

It was a small sombre room within, with a bare yellow-washed floor and ragged curtains at the little window. In a corner was a diminutive altar draped with threadbare lace. The red glow of the taper lighted a cheap print of St. Joseph and a brazen crucifix. The human element in the room was furnished by a little, wizened yellow woman, who, black-robed, turbaned, and stern, sat before an uncertain table whereon were greasy cards.

Manuela paused, her eyes blinking at the semi-obscurity within. The Wizened One called in croaking tones:

"An' fo' w'y you come here? Assiez-là, ma'amzelle."

Timidly Manuela sat at the table facing the owner of the voice.

"I want," she began faintly; but the Mistress of the

Cards understood: she had had much experience. The cards were shuffled in her long grimy talons and stacked before Manuela.

"Now you cut dem in t'ree part, so—un, deux, trois, bien! You mek' you' weesh wid all you' heart, bien! Yaas, I see, I see!"

Breathlessly did Manuela learn that her lover was true, but "dat light gal, yaas, she mek' nouvena in St. Rocque fo' hees love."

"I give you one lil' charm, yaas," said the Wizened One when the séance was over, and Manuela, all white and nervous, leaned back in the rickety chair. "I give you one lil' charm fo' to ween him back, yaas. You wear h'it 'roun' you' wais', an' he come back. Den you mek prayer at St. Rocque an' burn can'le. Den you come back an' tell me, yaas. Cinquante sous, ma'amzelle. Merci. Good luck go wid you."

Readjusting her veil, Manuela passed out the little wicket gate, treading on air. Again the sun shone, and the breath of the swamps came as healthful sea-breeze unto her nostrils. She fairly flew in the direction of St. Rocque.

There were quite a number of persons entering the white gates of the cemetery, for this was Friday, when all those who wish good luck pray to the saint, and wash their steps promptly at twelve o'clock with a wondrous mixture to guard the house. Manuela bought a candle from the keeper of the little lodge at the entrance, and pausing one instant by the great sun-dial to see if the heavens and the hour were propitious, glided into the tiny chapel, dim and stifling with heavy air from myriad wish-candles blazing on the wide table before the altar-rail. She said her prayer and lighting her candle placed it with the others.

Mon Dieu! how brightly the sun seemed to shine now, she thought, pausing at the door on her way out. Her small finger-tips, still bedewed with holy water, rested caressingly on a gamin's head. The ivy which enfolds the quaint chapel never seemed so green; the shrines which serve as the Way of the Cross never seemed so artistic; the baby graves, even, seemed cheerful.

Theophilé called Sunday. Manuela's heart leaped. He had been spending his Sundays with Claralie. His stay was short and he was plainly bored. But Manuela knelt to thank the good St. Rocque that night, and fondled the charm about her slim waist. There came a box of bonbons during the week, with a decorative card all roses and fringe, from Theophilé; but being a Creole, and therefore superstitiously careful, and having been reared by a wise and experienced maman to mistrust the gifts of a recreant lover, Manuela quietly thrust bonbons, box, and card into the kitchen fire, and the Friday following placed the second candle of her nouvena in St. Rocque.

Those of Manuela's friends who had watched with indignation Theophilé gallantly leading Claralie home from High Mass on Sundays, gasped with astonishment when the next Sunday, with his usual bow, the young man offered Manuela his arm as the worshippers filed out in step to the organ's march. Claralie tossed her head as she crossed herself with holy water, and the pink in her cheeks was brighter than usual.

Manuela smiled a bright good-morning when she

met Claralie in St. Rocque the next Friday. The little blonde blushed furiously, and Manuela rushed post-haste to the Wizened One to confer upon this new issue.

"H'it ees good," said the dame, shaking her turbaned head. "She ees 'fraid, she will work, mais you' charm, h'it weel beat her."

And Manuela departed with radiant eyes.

Theophilé was not at Mass Sunday morning, and murderous glances flashed from Claralie to Manuela before the tinkling of the Host-Bell. Nor did Theophilé call at either house. Two hearts beat furiously at the sound of every passing footstep, and two minds wondered if the other were enjoying the beloved one's smiles. Two pair of eyes, however, blue and black, smiled on others, and their owners laughed and seemed none the less happy. For your Creole girls are proud, and would die rather than let the world see their sorrows.

Monday evening Theophilé, the missing, showed his rather sheepish countenance in Manuela's parlour, and explained that he, with some chosen spirits, had gonc for a trip—"over the Lake."

"I did not ask you where you were yesterday," replied the girl, saucily.

Theophilé shrugged his shoulders and changed the conversation.

The next week there was a birthday fête in honour of Louise, Theophilé's young sister. Everyone was bidden, and no one thought of refusing, for Louise was young, and this would be her first party. So, though the night was hot, the dancing went on as merrily as light young feet could make it go. Claralie fluffed her dainty white skirts, and cast mischievous sparkles in the direction of Theophilé, who with the maman and Louise was bravely trying not to look self-conscious. Manuela, tall and calm and proud-looking, in a cool, pale yellow gown was apparently enjoying herself without paying the slightest attention to her young host.

"Have I the pleasure of this dance?" he asked her finally, in a lull of the music.

She bowed assent, and as if moved by a common impulse they strolled out of the dancing-room into the cool, quaint garden, where jessamines gave out an overpowering perfume, and a caged mocking-bird complained melodiously to the full moon in the sky.

It must have been an engrossing tête-a-tête, for the call to supper had sounded twice before they heard and hurried into the house. The march had formed with Louise radiantly leading on the arm of papa. Claralie tripped by with Leon. Of course, nothing remained for Theophilé and Manuela to do but to bring up the rear, for which they received much good-natured chaffing.

But when the party reached the dining-room, Theophilé proudly led his partner to the head of the table, at the right hand of maman, and smiled benignly about at the delighted assemblage. Now you know, when a Creole young man places a girl at his mother's right hand at his own table, there is but one conclusion to be deduced therefrom.

If you had asked Manuela, after the wedding was over, how it happened, she would have said nothing, but looked wise.

If you had asked Claralie, she would have laughed and said she always preferred Leon.

If you had asked Theophilé, he would have wondered that you thought he had ever meant more than to tease Manuela.

If you had asked the Wizened One, she would have offered you a charm.

But St. Rocque knows, for he is a good saint, and if you believe in him and are true and good, and make your nouvenas with a clean heart, he will grant your wish.

M

MACMILLAN COLLECTOR'S LIBRARY

All the books in this series:

A Carnival Jangle by Alice Dunbar Nelson

A Little Cloud by James Joyce

An Unwritten Novel by Virginia Woolf

The Home-Coming by Rabindranath Tagore

Jack and Alice by Jane Austen

The Curious Case of Benjamin Button
by F. Scott Fitzgerald

The Daughters of the Late Colonel
by Katherine Mansfield

The Murders in the Rue Morgue
by Edgar Allan Poe

The Nightingale and the Rose by Oscar Wilde

The Speckled Band by Arthur Conan Doyle